Shark in the Park!

For Lily

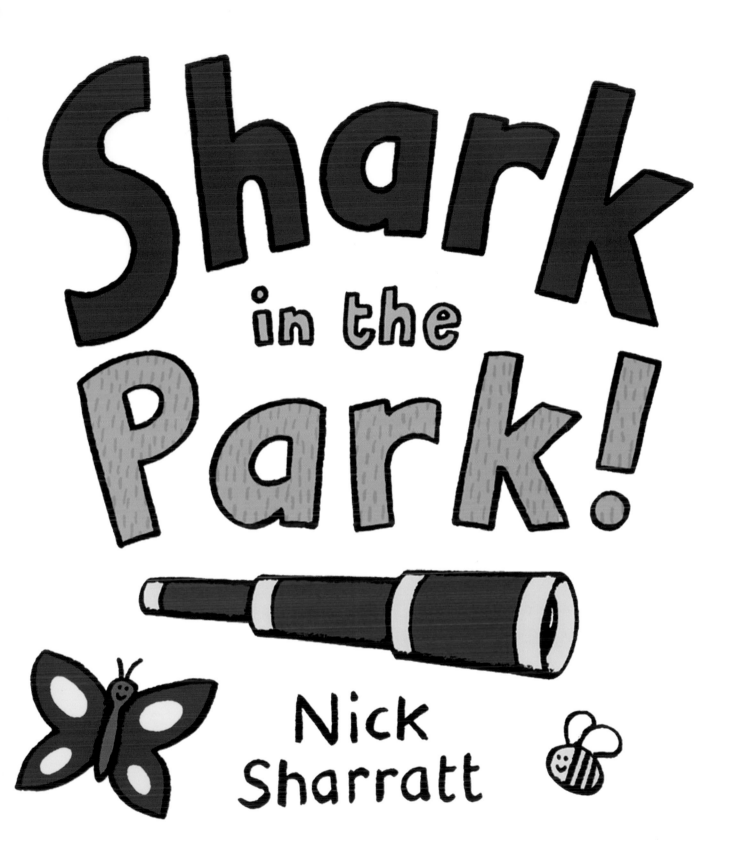

Shark
in the
Park!

Nick
Sharratt

PICTURE CORGI

Down at the park,
a little boy
is testing out
his brand new toy.

Timothy Pope, Timothy Pope
is looking through his telescope.

He looks at
the sky.

He looks at
the ground.

He looks
left and
right.

He looks all around.

Timothy Pope, Timothy Pope
looks again through his telescope.

He looks at
the sky.

He looks
left and
right.

He looks at
the ground.

He looks all around.

Timothy Pope, Timothy Pope
has one more look through
his telescope.

He looks at
the sky.

He looks at
the ground.

He looks
left and
right.

He looks all around.

SHARK IN THE PARK
A PICTURE CORGI BOOK 978 0 552 54977 6

First published in an educational format in 2000 by
Reed Educational & Professional Publishing Ltd
David Fickling Books edition published 2002
Picture Corgi edition published 2007

21

Picture Corgi Books are published by Random House Children's Publishers UK,
61–63 Uxbridge Road, London W5 5SA,
A RANDOM HOUSE GROUP COMPANY
Addresses for companies within The Random House Group Limited
can be found at: www.randomhouse.co.uk/offices.htm

THE RANDOM HOUSE GROUP Limited Reg. No. 954009
www.randomhousechildrens.co.uk

A CIP catalogue record for this book is available from the British Library.

Printed in China

More picture books illustrated
by Nick Sharratt:

PANTS

written by Giles Andreae

YOU CHOOSE

written by Pippa Goodhart

The Daisy books

written by Kes Gray:

006 AND A BIT

DOUBLE TROUBLE

A BUNCH OF DAISIES

YUK!

YOU DO!

REALLY, REALLY

EAT YOUR PEAS